FALL

INTO

MADNESS

PART 1

THE FALL

DEVISED BY:

JOHNATHAN RONIGER

Chapter One

Section A:

The Patrol

The brakes squeaked as the Up-Armored Humvee, carrying Specialist Elijah Two-Crows the driver, Sergeant First Class Jacklyn Price the truck commander, Staff Sergeant

Emmanuel Gutierrez the rear left passenger, Private Michael Marland the gunner, and Sergeant John White the rear right passenger, came to a stop at an intersection a mile from the main gate of Fort Jericho. It had been five years since the invasion and the team was conducting their weekly patrol around the Fort which is located in California in the area known as the Mojave Desert.

The invasion happened on March 15, 2015 with absolutely no warning. Within the year the hostiles had all but wiped out the U.S. Armed Forces. Small pockets of the military survived along with small portions of civilians taking shelter in bases and forts around the country. Those who were unable to take cover were exposed to an agent only known as the Madness for its effect on the human brain making them go insane. There was no way of knowing who all had survived due to the severance of communication between the military instillations and the world.

The team took a left along their usual route when Price noticed something in the distance. Unsure of what it was she had Two-Crows bring the Humvee to a halt then her, Gutierrez, and White dismounted the vehicle to investigate the anomaly. As the three soldiers approached the object Marland began to pull security with the Humvee's mounted fifty caliber machine gun. Slowly the object took shape and revealed itself to them. "It's a hostile." White said as they came upon the deceased being lying face down in the sand and rocks.

"Still fresh." Price announced as she examined the body.

"Think it was the heat?" Gutierrez asked crouching next to Price.

"Possibly."

"Hey guys!" White called who was standing fifteen feet away.

"What is it?" Responded Price as her and Gutierrez stood up and walked towards him.

"Looks like we have a Ravager presence." He answered picking up a tribal like spear.

"Maybe they are what killed the hostile." Ventured Gutierrez, attempting to tie one to the other.

"Could be." Price responded. "We need to.." She was cut off abruptly by the sound of a Ravager's bloodthirsty Hunting Howl grabbing the whole team's attention. "...go." She finished after the howl stopped. The three rushed back to the Humvee. Once they were inside, Price ordered Two-Crows to put some distance between them and the area. As they grew further from the scene Price radioed the tower to inform them of the Ravager presence. "Tower this is Metal-Head One over."

"This is Tower go ahead." Said a voice on the radio.

"Tower we have discovered a Ravager Hunting Scout about a mile from the Main Gate along with a deceased Hostile."

"Roger, Ravager presence and deceased Hostile noted."

"Shall we continue our patrol?"

"That is affirmative."

"Roger. Metal-Head One out." Price replied hanging the radio on the transceiver and telling Two-Crows to proceed along their usual route.

The Ravagers began to appear six months after the invasion started. They are believed to be the mass amount of people who were unable to find shelter and were exposed to the Hostiles' Madness Agent. They are insane and practice cannibalism. They are divided into multiple tribes. Each tribe can contain anywhere from twenty to a hundred Ravagers. The tribes are governed by a single chief. Each chief is decided by strength and must be able to kill the current chief in hand to hand combat.

They use a wide variety of weapons such as; spears, hatchets, and spiked clubs. They only use guns and explosives when encountering another tribe or attacking a larger prey like the military. Their language has become nothing more than simple phrases and grunts due to the Madness Agent's effect on their neurological processing. The 'Hunting Howl' is their most feared sound for it is used by a scout to signal a hunting party that food has been located. A Ravager Hunting Party proves to be efficient and deadly, but nowhere near as deadly as their War Parties. The War Party is to never be taken lightly.

"I'm so tired of this route." Two-Crows said breaking the silence that had grown in the Humvee.

"Oh stop your bitchin'." Price responded playfully. "You could always go back to gate guard."

"Fuck that and I ain't bitchin'." He chuckled "I was just sayin'."

"Sure sounded like bitching to me."

"Yeah, yeah fuck off." Two-Crows replied with a smile.

"You good back there White?" Price asked as her laughing subsided and she noticed his unusual quietness.

"Yeah, just thinking." White answered as he continued to plan his daughter Anna's birthday surprise. She had just turned five.

"What do you think of the Ravagers being that close to Jericho?" asked Gutierrez.

"Nothing much." White replied irritated as his thoughts were once again interrupted. "They aren't stupid enough to take on a fully equipped base."

"You never know."

"True." Said White returning his mind to his daughter.

Fort Jericho was originally known only as a training facility for units preparing to deploy. It was constructed on February 20, 1998. It wasn't ever designed to be able to withstand a full assault until recently unknown to most it now contains the last known Atomic Bomb. The bomb was moved there immediately following the invasion. Once it became known that the Hostiles grew strength from feeding off the bombs' radiation the U.S. began dismantling the bombs. Jericho sits on the last one. This caused Jericho to become a fully equipped facility. Though its defenses have eroded and slowly dwindled and is now unsuited to hold off a large assault by an enemy and will most likely overrun.

The team was becoming exhausted for it was the hottest time of the year in the Mojave. So after rounding two more turns Price had Two-Crows stop so they could stretch their legs and refuel the Humvee, with the spare fuel canister attached to the rear of the vehicle.

White and Gutierrez were the first to dismount the vehicle and headed towards the tail end to retrieve the fuel. As they came around the sides they both noticed something was wrong. "Price!" Yelled Gutierrez discovering the canister had been damaged and drained completely dry.

Price hopped out and rushed over to where White and Gutierrez were both standing. "What's wrong?" She asked just before noticing the problem. "Damn-it." She said as she knelt down to investigate what caused the damage.

"What happened?" asked White.

"Looks like it was sabotaged by a Ravager." Price answered as she removed a fragment of a hatchet from the lining of the canister. "Must've happened when we heard the Hunting Howl. Two-Crows how much fuel is left?"

"Just enough to make it to the Fort, but not enough to complete the patrol." He responded.

"Sergeant!" Marland exclaimed. "Incoming on our right!" The three turned to see a small Hunting Party running towards them. They quickly re-entered the Humvee. Price then ordered Two-Crows to return to the Fort.

The tires kicked up sand as they began to spin, but before they could move the Humvee was flipped over violently by an explosive thrown by one of the charging Ravagers.

Chapter One

Section B:

Fort Jericho

"Tower this is Metal-Head One over." Said Price over the radio.

"This is Tower go ahead." Responded Lieutenant Lawrence Jacobs.

"Tower we have discovered a Ravager Hunting Scout about a mile from the Main Gate along with a deceased Hostile."

"Roger, Ravager presence and deceased Hostile noted."

"Shall we continue our patrol?"

"That is affirmative."

"Roger. Metal-Head One out." Price replied. Jacobs then hung the radio on the transceiver and turned towards Staff Sergeant Derrick Willis who was stationed in the tower with him.

"Got any special plans tonight?" Jacobs asked as he finished writing up the report.

"Man, I'm probably going to grab me a 12 pack of Bud light from the store and that cute cashier I've been talking to and forgetting the day." Willis answered.

"That hot Hispanic girl?"

"You know it Bro."

"Sounds like a good plan." Jacobs grinned. Then like the voice of God the tower shook from a thunderous boom. "What the hell was that?" Jacobs exclaimed as the two of them ran to the window.

"Oh my God." They both uttered in unison watching hundreds of Ravagers spilling through a hole that had been blasted in the outer wall. Then before either one of them could react the tower was ripped apart by a shell fired from a rust covered Abrams tank that had rolled through the hole behind the Ravagers. The tower crumbled to the desert floor killing the two men.

"Move, move, move!" Ordered Captain Jake Piper as troops pooled out of the barracks and towards the wall wearing their full battle gear and M4's. "We have a Ravager War Party to eliminate." He said following the last ten soldiers out. The soldiers took cover and began firing at the Ravagers. Terror filled their hearts as they watched their fellow comrades having their skin torn from their bodies and devoured.

Piper watched as the men placed under his command getting beaten and ripped to shreds. "Keep pushing!" He yelled attempting to rally what was left of his men. Piper killed three more Ravagers before calling to his troops "We have to keep our people safe. Prove that they were right to tru..." he was suddenly cut off by a spear, thrown by the Ravagers' Chief who stood on top of the tank, tore through his neck decapitating the terrified captain.

The few remaining troops began to retreat after watching their leader being brought down, but their attempts failed as one by one the soldiers of the First Line fell to the bloodthirsty hoard.

"Feast-On-You-Shall-We!" Howled the Chief as the tank he stood upon rolled over the dead, crushing them into the dirt before being eaten by the Ravagers following behind it. "Shall-Not-Stop!" He began to chant. Then slowly the entire War Party chimed in and continued to chant as they butchered soldier after soldier. It wasn't long before the Second Line under the command of Captain Reece Clark fell to the Ravager hoard. Clark's cries of pain as he was ripped apart filled the air causing those who heard it to know fear and hopelessness.

"Hold Fast!" Yelled General Benjamin Brock, who was the commander of Fort Jericho and in charge of the third and final defensive line. "Do not be afraid. They are only animals. You can beat them." He continued in his attempt to rally his troops together. He could see the fear in their eyes as they heard the ominous chant growing louder and louder by the second. He took a deep breath and then began to give his men an uplifting speech.

"We are the last line of defense. Countless women, children, and men are depending on this line to hold. On you to hold. Do not let them down and do not let your brothers sacrifices be in vain. Yes they outnumber us and yes they are strong. But you are stronger than all of them combined. You have the courage and the will to overpower the madness that knocks at our door. You just have to believe in something worth fighting for. If you can muster the belief then nothing can stop you. We will be victorious today. We will prove our might. We will prove our courage. We will prove our will. And most importantly. We will prove to everyone that the light will always shine through the darkness and destroy the madness!."

The moment Brock's speech concluded the soldiers erupted in a thunderous roar that for a second overpowered the Ravagers' chant and was heard across the entire Fort. Brock watched as the War Party broke through the last barrier and ferociously charged him and his men. Gunshots rang out across the Fort as the General and the others began firing upon the hoard.

The Ravagers quickly retaliated as several of them that had been carrying rifles began to return fire. For every five Ravagers killed a soldier was lost. It wasn't long before Brock was down to only a handful of men. They seemed endless for no matter how many the soldiers killed the Ravagers just kept coming.

Brock watched as the beasts overpowered his men and removed

them from the battlefield piece by piece. His ammunition was running low and he was now down to his sidearm. One after the other he killed the Ravagers until his weapon began to click empty. He then threw it at one of the creatures and charged in killing it with his bare hands.

He continued and struck down eight more until he was finally brought down by a surprise attack by one striking him from behind. Brock fell to the ground and was beaten as he watched the small portion of his men that were left be torn apart. Then he heard the sound of metal crunching bodies as it rolled closer. The machine stopped and he heard a beast of a voice say "Bring-Me." Then suddenly Brock was forced up and drug to the Animal that was standing on the machine.

After being thrown to the giant brute by a couple of Ravagers. He was picked up by his throat. Brock then stared into the creature's black soulless eyes. "You-Chief?" The brute asked. Brock refused to answer him, all he did was smile and spit the blood that had pooled in his mouth at him. The monster became enraged and let out a roar as he used his hand to tear Brock's face from his body then snapping his neck with the other hand.

The giant threw Brock's lifeless body to the Ravager hoard and placed the general's face upon his own. "Feast-Now." He said ordering the War Party to invade the Housing

District and feast on all who dwelled within. The Ravagers quickly moved into the District and began killing everyone in sight. The sound of blood curdling cries and Ravagers laughing filled the air. It was the sound of horror and true hopelessness to any and all who could hear. It announced the tragic fall of Fort Jericho and the failure of its fearless leader General Brock and all he stood for.

The murderous being that had killed Brock retired to the inside of the tank and removed the general's face. He then placed it alongside the countless leaders that opposed him before. Then as he gazed upon his trophies in pride he said a phrase that was rapidly coming true. "No-Hope," He paused and looked down

at Brocks bodiless face. "Madness-
Wins-Always."

Chapter One

Section C:

The Survivors

As the smoke around the Humvee cleared White awoke, his vision blurred and his ears ringing. As things came into focus he noticed that Two-Crows and Gutierrez were missing. He continued to look around for a moment before seeing what remained of Marland, he had been torn in half by the roll over. Then White heard something outside and when he looked he saw Two-Crows, who was being ripped apart and eaten by two Ravagers.

Just as he was beginning to think he was the last one left he heard Price cough herself into consciousness. "Shh," White sounded.

"They don't know we sur..." just then both of their doors opened and they were ripped from the vehicle by two more Ravagers. White winced as the bright desert sun shown in his eyes. As his vision cleared he saw he was being held down along with Price.

He then turned his attention to the fifth Ravager that was slowly approaching them with a blood covered rusty hatchet. White closed his eyed and began to picture his daughter for he wanted his last thought to a peaceful and joyous one. He took solace in knowing she was safe and sound in Housing District behind the fortified walls of Fort Jericho.

White tightened his eyelids together as he heard the

approaching Ravager's footsteps growing louder. Then suddenly as if an angel had been watching over him, White heard five gunshots and Price yelling at him to get up. Gutierrez had managed to escape before the Ravagers could reach the Humvee and fled to ready his weapon and himself. Unfortunately they got to Two-Crows before he could react. He wasn't about to allow anyone else to die.

White jumped up and regrouped with the other two who were discussing their next move. "We need to go back." Price said as White walked up.

"I agree." Gutierrez responded as he placed his rifle on safe.

"We are waisting daylight." White interrupted.

"And that can't be the only Hunting Party around." Price added as she retrieved her's and White's weapons from the Humvee.

"We should give them a proper burial first." White said taking the M4 Price had handed him.

"You're right." Price agreed. "Gutierrez help me with Two-Crows and White you get what you can of Marland out. After they buried and all said something over their fallen comrades the three quickly made their way back to Jericho.

The sun beat its heat against them as they topped the final rocky ridge. Each of their faces opened in terror as they saw the one thing they never expected to see. Fort Jericho had fallen to the Ravagers. Price quickly took her binoculars out from her cargo pocket and scanned the Fort to assess the damage. "Oh God." She uttered in a saddened tone.

"What is it?" Gutierrez ask.

"They killed General Brock." She answered as she watched Brock's face get removed by a large Ravager standing on top of a tank.

"Oh God." Echoed Gutierrez as he slumped to the dirt.

"What about the Housing District?" Questioned White "What about Anna?"

Price then looked towards the Housing District to see if she could find White's daughter. White watched as she scanned for a moment and then suddenly stopped on a fixed point. White noticed her mouth slowly open as if to say something, but nothing came out. "Well?" He rushed for an answer. After a few seconds of no response White took the binoculars from her and searched for the area she was viewing. It took only a moment before he found it.

"I'm so sorry White." Price said as she watched tears flow from his eyes.

White stood silent as he witnessed his daughter being torn limb from agonizing limb crying out for her father to save her. White felt a rush of cold numbness as his heart emptied of love and hope and was filled with sorrow and madness. He was only able to say one word. "Anna..." Then before Price could place a comforting hand on his shoulder he dropped the binoculars and started sprinting as fast as he could towards the Fort.

"White!" Yelled Price as her and Gutierrez chased after him. "White!"

Chapter Two

Section A:

White & Anna

"Daddy?" Said little Anna as she walked through the house looking for her father. They were playing a game of hide and seek. "Daddy?" She entered his bedroom and began searching under his bed and in his walk-in closet, but he was nowhere to be found.

She exited the room and crossed the hall to her room. She entered and began her search again. Finally she came to pink closet. As she opened it White jumped out and swooped her up. She let out a quick scream of shock and then almost immediately joined her father in laughter.

White dropped her in her bed and tickled her to the point of tears and then collapsed next to her on the bed. They laid there and laughed until the couldn't possibly laugh anymore. "Alright sweetheart it's time for bed. You have a big day tomorrow." White said as he sat up.

"Will you read me a story?" She asked in a tone that you could hear her smiling in.

"Of course. What would you like to hear?"

"Tell me the one of the princess and the brave knight."

"You got it." He said scooting back to lean on the headboard. Anna placed her head in his lap and prepared for the story. "Ready?"

"Yup." She replied.

"Alright. Here we go." He said as he took a breath. "Once in faraway land where dragons ruled the skies and kings ruled the lands. There was a Princess who was about to turn five."

"Like me?!" Anna interrupted as she usually does at this part.

"Yes just like you." Answered White, "She was born in the land of Jericho ruled by King Brock her father. One day while the King and his army were away fighting dragons the castle was attacked by a band of Raiders."

"Darn Raiders." She commented balling her tiny hand into a fist.

White smiled and then continued. "As this was happening the Princess, Princess Anna." Anna smiled for she knew it was her. "Was very scared so she ran from the castle but was captured by the Raiders. Then suddenly as though lightning shot from the sky a brave White Knight galloped in on his mighty steed and fought off the Raiders. Saving the Princess. After the Raiders had fled in terror the Knight climbed down from his horse and helped Princess Anna to her feet. After dusting her off carefully and gently the King and his army rode in ready for battle. The King sighed in great relief as he saw his daughter was safe. 'Oh thank you kind Knight. I don't know what I would do without my daughter.' Said the King as he picked Anna up and held her in his arms. 'It was my honor Sire.' The Knight replied. He then turned towards the Princess and said 'I promise that for as long as I live I will keep you safe from harm.' And he kept his promise and the Princess and the kingdom were safe thanks to the brave White Knight. The End." White looked and smiled as he saw Anna fast asleep on his lap.

He gently placed her head on her princess patterned pillow and tucked her safely under the covers. He then leaned down and kissed her forehead and just before exiting the room he turned and said "I promise that as long as I live I will never let any harm come to you Anna. I love you." He then continued to exit the room and head to his to sleep.

The next morning Anna awoke to the smell of blueberry pancakes, her favorite, and the sound of soldiers moving through Fort Jericho on their usual rounds and duties. She arose from her bed and headed towards the kitchen. As she neared the dining room she could hear her father humming her favorite song 'Somewhere over the Rainbow'.

She walked into the dining room to see his and her plate setting on the table with breakfast already prepared and waiting on her. "Hey sweetheart." White said exiting the kitchen. "Sleep well?" he asked as they sat down. He was dressed in his military uniform for it was the day he went on patrol with Price and the others in his team. "So I know it's your birthday so I was able to get our patrol time pushed so I can take you to Supermart to get a present."

"Okay." She said in her usual sweet cheerful voice as she began eating.

After they were finished White cleaned up as Anna got dressed in her blue jeans and pink 'Daddy's Princess' shirt. They then headed to Supermart. They shopped around until Anna stopped and pointed a play castle with a knight and princess. "I want that one." She said, "It's just like your story."

"Anything for you." White replied with a big smile as he took it off the shelf.

"Let's go home so I can play with it."

"Yes ma'am." He said playfully as they went to the cashier. After they got home White watched as Anna took the castle to her room. "Okay Debbie is here." He announced as Anna's babysitter pulled into the drive way. Anna came charging out of the room and wrapped herself around White as he knelt down to give her a hug. "I'll see you the moment I get off patrol."

"Promise?" She asked letting go.

"I promise." White responded kissing her forehead and standing up.

"Okay, I love you Daddy."

"I love you too my little Princess Anna."

She gave him a huge smile and then returned to her room. White then turned and opened the door for Debbie. "Thank you Mister White." She said entering the house.

"No problem, take good care of her for me."

"I will."

"I'll be back shortly." White responded exiting the house. He trekked his way to the main gate and met up with the rest of the team.

"Ready?" Asked Price.

"Ready." Answered White as the two of them entered the Humvee.

"She's growing up fast." Price commented as Two-Crows started the engine.

"She sure is. She looks just like her mother."

"Donna would be proud of you."

"I hope so." Replied White as the Humvee exited the Fort and turned right.

Chapter
Two

Section B:

What Remains

"White!" Price continued to shout as her and Gutierrez was chasing White. Before they knew it they had entered Fort Jericho. As they lost sight of White through the houses they noticed a small group containing fifteen civilians sneaking from house to house to evade the carnivorous animals that now roamed the base.

"Price." Gutierrez said he stopped running. "We have to help them."

"What about White?" She asked stopping and turning towards him.

"I'd hate to say it but he's trained enough to take care of himself."

"He's not thinking straight."

"I know but they will die if we don't help them."

"And where do you suppose we take them? We barely have enough supplies for ourselves let alone fifteen others."

"I know of a base." Gutierrez replied. "It's about a day's walk from here. If we go now we can make it before we even need to worry about supplies.”

“How do you know about this place?” Price asked “And why didn’t you mention it before?”

“I sometimes go for hikes outside the Fort and on one of those hikes I saw it in the distance. At first I thought it was abandoned but on our patrol I was looking through my binoculars and I could see Military personnel, but before I could say anything we were attacked.”

“So we get those people there and then what?” Price said in an aggravated tone. “We hope they take us in and help us get White back?”

"It's our best option to save these people and ourselves." He responded.

Price looked back in the direction White had been running then turned back to Gutierrez and said "Let's get moving then." In a regretful tone.

The two of them walked to where they were visible to the civilians. "Hey!" called Gutierrez getting their attention. "Follow us. We can get you to safety." Then like a herd of gazelle running from a lion they all ran towards him and Price.

"Let's go." Price said as they began to lead them out of Fort Jericho and into the Mojave.

"Where are we going?" asked a man who seemed to have been

leading the group before Price and Gutierrez came along.

"There is another military instillation about a day's walk from here." Gutierrez answered. "You will be safe there Mister?"

"The name's Crawford. Aaron Crawford." replied the man. "And no offense, but that's what they said about Fort Jericho and you see where that lead us."

"Look." Intervened Price. "What happened here was a freak incident. It will not happen again. We will be better prepared next time. Now if that's all I'd like to get us as far away from Jericho as possible before nightfall."

"I hope you're right." Said Crawford as they continued to trek through the desert. The arid sun beat against the group with every step they took. Soon seconds felt like minutes, minutes felt like hours, and each hour felt like an eternity.

"How far was this base again?" Price asked Gutierrez.

"About a day's walk like I said." He answered.

"How the hell did you just happen upon this place?"

"I sometimes go for hikes with my binoculars and just scan the area for any signs of life other than Ravagers. And on the last one I saw this place. That's about it." Gutierrez replied.

"And you sure you saw civilized people there?" Price asked taking a quick look back at the group and then returning her gaze forward.

"Yes. They wore uniforms and operated in a militaristic manner. Something the Ravagers seem incapable of."

"I hope your right." She said dropping the barrage of questions. "For all our sakes."

"Excuse me." Whispered a woman walking up to Crawford. "Mister Crawford?"

"Please, just Aaron." Crawford replied in the same hushed tone.

"Okay, Aaron what do you think of all this? Are we safe with them?"

"What's your name?"

"Shania Light."

"Well Shania I promise that as long as you stick close to me you'll be safe." Crawford said comforting the young woman.

"Okay. Thank you."

"It's no problem."

"Alright." Price said stopping. "We should make camp here and set out first thing tomorrow." The group didn't realize it was already becoming night. "Unfortunately due to the proximity to Jericho we can't risk a fire so we will have to group up and use our combined body heat to stay warm."

"What about food and water?" asked Crawford.

"Food and water will be available once we reach our

destination. Though for sake of dehydration Gutierrez and I will pass around our canteens."

"Alright everyone only drink enough to wet your mouths. Take too much and there won't be enough for everyone."

"Exactly." Price added, agreeing with Crawford.

"Women and children first." Crawford continued. After everyone had taken a drink they began to group together and lay on the ground. Not long after they all laid down the night filled the sky with a spectacular array of stars. One by one each member of the group drifted to sleep. Price was the last, taking one more look at the sky then

closing her eyes hoping the next day
would bring them better luck.

Chapter Two

Section C:

The Ruins of Jericho

As White charged the Fort he could hear Price yelling for him, but nothing mattered anymore. The only thing running through his mind was vengeance. The yelling ceased after he passed in between some buildings. Thinking he lost them he turned left and ran towards his house. He didn't want to wait for the other two for he knew they would just try to stop him.

As he neared the house he could see two Ravagers still eating parts of his daughter. His speed increased and rage heightened. Before they could react he attacked the Ravagers. He kicked one in the head knocking him down and tackled the other. White then relentlessly began beating the one he tackled to death.

After he was finished he stood and turned his anger towards the other one who was trying to flee. But before the Ravager could get up and run White grabbed his foot and drug him back. Then in a swift motion White broke the animal's leg and began stopping on his head with his combat boot until there was nothing but mangled flesh and bone in the sand.

After they were dead the anger and bloodthirst subsided and White turned to face what remained of Anna. His legs trembled as they weakened from the weight of his sorrow. He collapsed to his hands and knees with tears pouring from his eyes. He began to crawl towards her soaking the ground with each movement. He gathered her cold bloodied body in his arms and pressed her tight against his chest.

Her golden blonde hair grew wet from White's tears as they fell upon her head. His heart was filled with ache and confusion for it couldn't fathom the amount of sadness he was feeling. White couldn't say a word, all he could do was whimper because his teeth wouldn't unclench. Then after a moment he was finally able to speak due to his jaw tiring from the tension.

"I'm so very sorry sweetheart." He said in a broken tear-filled manner. "I broke my promise. I should have been here. I failed. Your brave knight failed you." Before he could say another word a flood of pain and tears interrupted him. "I'm sorry Donna." He said in between sobs talking to his wife, who died during child birth. "I failed to keep our little girl safe."

After several more minutes the tears began stop either from exhaustion or dehydration. White then in a crackled voice began to sing Anna's favorite song to her. "Somewhere over the rainbow. Way up high. There's a land that you dreamed of once in a lullaby..." the singing continued and could be heard for several blocks. The sound of pure misery and hopelessness filled the air. It was enough to cause even a Ravager to cry.

The stars lit the night sky and decorated it with a multitude of constellations. White sat there for a moment longer rocking back and fourth with Anna's body. He then stood up from the dirt and gently carried her into the house. When he entered he saw what little remained of Debbie strung throughout the kitchen as if she were the main course of a Viking feast.

'Poor girl.' White thought as he stepped over what seemed to be the remains of her small intestines. He made his way to Anna's room and then gently laid her body onto her still made bed. He took a step back and looked around to remember what it used to look like. As his foot touched the floor he felt something. He raised his bloodied boot and looked down to see the knight figurine from the toy castle he bought her.

He reached down and picked it up to look at it. After staring blankly at it for a few seconds trying to imagine what him and Anna were going to do when he had gotten off patrol. He then put the toy knight into his pocket and looked back at Anna. A small tear formed in his right eye and rolled down the curves of his face then dripped onto the wooden floor.

He moved forward and laid in the bed next to his still daughter. He looked into her shine-less eyes for a moment and then wrapped his arms around her once again. He pulled her close and held her as if he was trying to warm her cold body. Then before he knew it he had fallen asleep with her just like when she had a bad dream.

Chapter Three

Section A:

Birth & Death

"Hey honey." White said entering his wife's hospital room. "Here's some juice." He handed her a small paper cup of apple juice. After she accepted it from him he placed his hand on her swollen pregnant belly. "Won't be long now and we'll be parents."

"Anna." Donna said placing her soft gentle hand on his.

"What's that?" he asked watching her drink the juice and place the cup on the bedside table.

"I want to name her Anna. Anna Sheryl White. After your mother."

"Anna it is." White smiled at his beautiful wife and couldn't imagine anywhere better than by her side.

White's mother died when he was fifteen years old. His father went when he had just turned twenty six, three years ago. White often spoke of them, especially his mother, which is the reason he thinks she picked that name.

"I hate being pregnant." Donna said with a smile. "It sucks. Why can't babies get delivered by storks like in cartoons?"

"I'm sorry. My stork must have gotten confused and thought your womb was the front porch." White responded with a childlike grin following a wink.

"Those jokes will have to quit once Anna's here." She giggled.

"I love you."

"And I love you silly boy." Donna pushed a strand of her dark brown hair behind her ear, then suddenly her face went from one of joy to one of pain. "It's time!" She announced grabbing her stomach.

"I'll get the doctor." White said rushing out of the room and into the hallway. It was only seconds before he returned with her doctor. The Doctor quickly examined her and then gave the signal that it was time. Before he knew it several nurses entered the room.

"Okay, here we go." Said the Doctor as his head disappeared behind Donna's gown. "You ready?" he asked looking up at her. Donna was unable to speak due to the pain so she nodded her head up and down to say yes.

"Here we go honey." White said as they gripped one another's hand.

Donna's grip tightened as she managed to say "Promise me that if anything happens you'll protect our daughter." to White who had looked down at her.

"Baby nothing…"

"Promise me John!" She said interrupting him.

"I promise." He replied just before the Doctor ordered he to push.

"Push!" He said again as Donna yelled pushing again and again. "Again." The Doctor began to repeat several times before announcing "I can see the head. Push!"

Donna pushed and pushed until suddenly like a band of angelic trumpets the baby began to fill the room with cries of life. After the umbilical cord was cut the Doctor wrapped the infant in a pink blanket and handed her over to the parents. "Congratulations it's a baby girl."

"Our little princess Anna." Donna said with a huge smile. Then suddenly, as if the moment was too perfect for reality, Donna's heart monitor flat-lined and he head fell back against the pillow.

"Donna!" Yelled White in panic.

"Prep the O.R.!" yelled the Doctor as both him and two nurses sprang into action and wheeled

Donna out of the room. One of the nurses took hold of Anna so White could follow the Doctor.

White paced rapidly back and forth outside the operating room awaiting the Doctor to bring news. Then after another hour passed by the Doctor finally emerged. "Well?" questioned White impatiently.

"It seems your wife had internal bleeding due to the strain the birthing process had on her. We did all we could but..."

"Is my wife okay?" interrupted White.

"I'm sorry Mister White. Your wife's heart couldn't handle it. She didn't make it." Answered the Doctor placing his hand on White's shoulder.

White stood silent. The look of shock and heartache took hold and everything became inaudible to him. A tear fell from his eye and to the tile floor of the hospital. After another moment of stillness he turned and walked away from the Doctor and back to the room where the nurse was watching Anna.

He entered the room and the nurse exited for she knew what had happened from the look on his face. He took another step towards the crib they had placed Anna in and watched as she looked around. A sense of amazement was in her eyes as she was seeing the world for the first time. "She has your eyes." White said as if he were speaking to Donna. "Anna," he mumbled with a smile.

Then as if she had understood him she looked up and directly at White. His breath escaped his lungs for a moment and then as it returned so did the smile. White looked into his daughter's eyes and felt a sense of joy and peace. He felt as if Donna was standing alongside him and everything was going to be okay. "I promise I will always love and protect you little princess Anna." He said as another tear left his eye and rolled of the corner of his smile.

Chapter
Three

Section B:

A New Home

Price was woken by the early morning sun coming over the mountains in the distance and shining on her sunburnt face. She stood and dusted the sand from her uniform. As she looked around at the sleeping group she couldn't help but feel sad that White was not among them. She then watched as slowly one by one each member of the group woke up.

"Everyone ready?" She asked after the final one arose from ground.

"I believe so." Crawford answered.

"Let's go." Price turned and along with Gutierrez began heading towards the other base.

"Not much further now." Gutierrez added as everyone started to follow them.

The group trekked for another two hours before Gutierrez announced that they had arrived. As they came over the last hill they saw a base half the size of Jericho with approximately one hundred soldiers patrolling and operating inside its walls. "Come on." Said Gutierrez, leading the group to the base's front gate.

"Halt!" Ordered a guard standing behind the chain-link fence gate. "Identify yourselves."

"I'm Sergeant First Class Price." She answered. "We are survivors from Fort Jericho. We were overrun by Ravagers. We seek shelter and food." The guard stepped back from the gate and towards a parked Humvee. He reached inside, took hold of radio, and began talking into it.

After a few moments of conversation with the person on the other line the guard signaled the two men operating the gate's gears. The two then pulled a couple of levers then suddenly the gate screeched open. The group slowly entered only to be met by a dark haired man in a uniform. Price scanned his chest for rank and saw that he was a two star general.

"Hello there." The man said extending his hand in friendship. "I'm General Hood." He continued as Price took his hand. "But please call me Mathew." They shook each other's hand firmly and then released.

"Thank you for taking us in. We have been through a lot." Price said taking a step back.

"It's no problem. I'm just glad you are all alright. You are all welcomed here, we have plenty of food and fresh water." He said to the group as another slightly taller man approached. "This is Captain Timothy Clifford." Hood put his hand on the man's shoulder. "Follow him. He will take you to your quarters. Please let me know if there is anything we can do to assist you further."

The group began to follow Clifford, all but Price who stayed behind to talk to Hood. "There is something else." She said as Hood looked away from the group and back at her.

"Whatever it is I'll do my best to accommodate it."

"Before we found them there were three of us. One fell behind. His name is John White."

"And you'd like my assistance to get him back?"

"I would greatly appreciate it."

"Let me see what I can do. I'll get with you in the morning. You need rest Sergeant."

"I know. I'll see you first thing?"

"First thing." Hood replied. "Now please get some rest."

"I'll see you in the morning then." Price said before returning to the group. They followed Clifford to a large shell shaped tent. As they entered they saw several cots set up with blankets and pillows. Each cot had an MRE and full canteen on it.

The group started picking cots and began eating. As Price took a drink of the canteen on her cot

Crawford walked up. "Sergeant Price." He said. "Me and my family would like to thank you."

"It's no problem." She answered. Crawford smiled and then returned to his family. Price placed both the MRE and the canteen on the concrete flooring and laid down on the cot. She pulled the blanket over her after removing her coat and boots. She stared up at the tent's ceiling for a moment and thought of White, wondering if he was alright and what he might be going through at that time. Then she began thinking of when General Brock had gotten her into Fort Jericho. Before she knew it she was asleep.

Chapter

Three

Section C:

Brock & Fort Jericho

"Hold on!" Staff Sergeant Willis called to Price as she began to slip from the cliff they were climbing. Willis slowly worked his way over to her position and extended his hand. "Give me your hand."

"Got it." Price said taking hold of his hand. Willis then pulled her up to the next ledge where she quickly reclaimed her grip and released his hand.

"You two alright?" asked Brock who was a few feet above them.

"Yeah we got it." Willis replied as they all continued to climb. Brock was the first to reach the top. After checking for any enemies or creatures he turned and began aiding the other two up.

"Good?" He asked helping Price up.

"Yeah." She responded as she gained her footing.

"Alright, not much further."

"Hope this place is as safe as you say."

"It is." Brock answered leading them onward. The three of them hiked for another two hours before finally reaching their destination.

"Halt!" ordered a guard by the main gate.

"My name is General Benjamin Brock and we have come across the Mojave to seek refuge inside Fort

Jericho." Brock said as a heavy set man approached the gate.

"I'm Colonel Joseph Peterson and I am in command over this instillation." The man said stopping at the gate. "I'm sorry General but our gates are closed."

"What do you mean closed?" Brock asked taking a step forward.

"No one else is permitted to enter the Fort."

"But we are people. Innocent people who just seek shelter."

"It doesn't matter. You are not the first to be turned away and you will not be the last."

"Listen to me." Brock bolstered. "We are human beings just like you. I'd let you in. If you turn us away you might as well give free entry to the Ravagers for that is what you would become. No. Worst. You would become Hostiles. I'd even allow a Ravager to enter if he needed it in order to survive. To turn us or anyone away is to give up on your humanity and hope. If we give up on hope we will embrace madness. I will not allow anyone to fall to the madness. Not even you. If you allow the madness to win then every death and sacrifice made was in vain. We are people just like you and deserve equal treatment. We cannot give up. I will not give up. So I say open the damn gate or madness take you." Just as Brock finished his speech the gate began to open.

"What are you doing soldier!?" Peterson yelled at the guard.

"I'm letting them in." the guard replied as the three entered the Fort. "My name is Elijah Two-Crows and I am with you to the end sir."

"I welcome you Elijah and you have my thanks." Brock answered.

"My name is Michael Marland!" shouted the guard standing opposite of Two-Crows. "And to hell with madness!"

"Damn right Marland."

"You can't just walk in here." Cried Peterson as Brock stepped up to him. Then like thunder Brock stuck Peterson knocking him to the ground.

"I'm in charge of this instillation now." Brock said helping Peterson to his feet. "Now show these two to their quarters."

"Yes sir." Peterson whimpered holding his bleeding nose.

"Go with him." Brock looked over his shoulder at Price and Willis. "He won't cause you any problems."

"Yes sir." The two replied in unison as they started to follow Peterson.

"Two-Crows, Marland. Take me to your Head Quarters." Brock said to the two guards who helped him get into Jericho.

"You got it." Two-Crows responded as him and Marland joined up with the General and began to lead him to the H.Q.

Chapter Four

Section A:

Return to Jericho

Price awoke as the sun was just hitting the tent causing it to light up in and orange-like color. She looked around to see the group was still asleep, then she noticed Hood approaching her. "There you are." He said reaching her cot. "How'd you sleep?"

"Not too bad." She replied sitting up and grabbing her jacket.

"Well I have bad news and I have good news."

"What's the bad?" Price slowly put on her jacket and then grabbed the half full canteen she had placed beside the cot.

"Bad news is I couldn't get a team together due to how stretched thin we are."

"And the good news?" She replied after finishing off the water in the canteen.

"Good news is that I'm coming with you." Hood answered watching Price set the canteen down and start to put her boots back on. "So when you're ready just let me know and we'll head out."

"Let's not waste any time then." She said tying her boots and standing up.

"Alright, I'll go get some supplies. Meet me out by the gate when you are set."

"Will do." Price answered. Hood then turned and walked away. "We're coming White. Just hold on a little longer." She mumbled as she put the MRE into her bag and went to refill her canteen.

After the canteen was refilled she began heading towards the gate when she was stopped by Gutierrez. "You going after White?" he asked running up to her.

"Yes." She replied.

"I'm coming with you."

"No." she placed her hand on his shoulder. "I need you here to watch over the group while I'm gone. I'll be fine."

"Okay. Be careful, and bring our boy back." Gutierrez said just before returning to the tent. Price continued on her way to meet up with Hood.

"Ready?" Hood asked as she walked up.

"Yes." She responded. Hood then signaled the guards to open the gate just far enough for them to get out. Once they were out the gate closed and they started their journey back to Jericho.

"So I have to ask." Hood said breaking the silence that had grown between them. "Why are you so intent on getting him back? I mean I know he's a fellow soldier and all but this seems a bit more than that. Were you and White an item?"

"I don't see how that would be any of your business." She answered shooting down Hood's question.

"Okay, didn't mean to pry." They topped a hill. "So what happened to Brock?"

"He died fighting the Ravagers. The way I see it those people back at the tent wouldn't be there if it wasn't for him."

"That man was quite the fighter."

"And a great leader."

"So I've heard." Hood responded. "I heard he practically made Fort Jericho into the beacon of hope it was."

"How did you hear all that?" Price asked as they crossed over a small patch of dead grass.

"I use to live in Jericho before I decided to set out to find more. My plan was to bring people back to Jericho but I ended up finding Fort Baxter and staying there instead. We stayed in contact Brock and I. He always made sure I wasn't turning anyone away." The two topped another hill.

"That was Brock." Price said. "Somehow no matter how bad things got he always had hope and wanted to share it. I guess that's what made him so great."

"That and those speeches of his." Hood chuckled.

"Yeah he loved to inspire people." She agreed with a smile.

The two continued their trek for several more hours before the sun began to set behind the mountains. "It'll be dark soon." Hood said as their speed slowed due to the decrease in visibility.

"We can make camp here and set out first thing in the morning." Price replied as the slowed to a stop.

"I brought two pop up tents and sleeping bags for us." Hood took off his ruck. "Here you go." He handed a tent and sleeping bag to her.

"Thanks." She said taking them. It only took a minute for them to set up the tents and place the sleeping bags inside.

"See you in the morning." Hood said climbing into his and zipping up the tent's entrance.

"Goodnight." Price replied doing the same. Soon they were both sound asleep.

Chapter Four

Section B:

Savages

White woke up to the sun seeping through his daughter's window curtains casting a pink light in the room. He unclenched Anna's body and slowly stood up. He tucked the covers in around her and stood in mourning for a moment before hearing the sound of a woman screaming not too far away.

White leaned over and gave Anna one last kiss on her forehead and then leapt into action, charging out of the house. He stopped for a moment and waited for another scream to tell him which direction to go. She cried out once again allowing White to follow the sound.

As he rounded another corner he stopped. He had found the source of the terror filled shrieks. It was a woman being held down with her clothes torn from her. She was being violently raped by a pack of Ravagers. "Savages." White said under his breath as the site had him frozen in place.

After a second of stillness he rushed in to save her from her torment. Before he knew it White had drop kicked the Ravager who was in the process of sexually assaulting the poor woman. White quickly jumped to his feet retrieving the combat knife from his boot and cut open one of the ones holding her leg's throat. The Ravager's blood spilled soaking the sand around him.

White felt one grab his shoulder but before the Ravager could do anything White spun around and stabbed him in the abdomen and continued the process until the Ravager fell dead. White then turned his attention to the other two who had released the woman and were now charging him.

He threw his knife into the eye of one, killing him, and in a swift and clean motion broke the other one's neck. As the Ravager fell White saw the one he had drop kicked attempting to crawl away. White approached the animal after retrieving his knife and grabbed the Ravager's arm. White then rolled him over to where he was facing the sky and proceeded to plunge the knife into his genitals. White continued this motion until the Ravager's eyes grew dark with death and then arose to see to the woman.

"Are you okay?" White asked extending his hand to the woman who was cowering against a wall.

"Are they gone?" She replied in a tearful tone.

"Yes, they are gone." The woman slowly took his hand and was helped to her feet.

"Thank you." She whimpered as White wrapped his jacket around her pale bruised body.

"You are going to be okay." He said wiping a tear from her cheek. "I promise." They began slowly walking away from the area.

"Okay." White placed his arm around her to help her stay up.

"What's your name?" he asked, but before she was able to answer White heard a loud thud and watched as the woman fell to the ground. Killed from being impaled in the back of the head by a hatchet. White turned around to see a large group of Ravagers standing behind him. "I'll kill you all. And then your Chief!" he yelled preparing to charge. But before he could take a single step a net was thrown on top of him knocking him to the ground.

In a matter of seconds the Ravagers circled around him and began collaborating their next move. "He-Challenge-Chief." One said. "Bring-To-Chief." Said another. They then howled in agreement. "First-We-Wait-For-Sun." one responded noticing that night was coming.

"What-We-Do-With-Challenge?"

"Leave-Here."

"What-If-Flee?"

White watched as one approached him with their rifle drawn. "He-No-Go-Anywhere." Said the Ravager just before using the butt-stock of the rifle to knock White unconscious.

Chapter
Four

Section C:

A Final Memory

Price laughed along with White at a story he was telling, about him and his little brother, before they both took another drink of the left over wine from the night's dinner. "You are something else John." She said placing the now empty glass down on the bar that divided the kitchen from the dining room.

"You are quite something as well." He replied refilling both of their glasses. "So it's been a year since we started dating."

"So it has." She answered in a provocative tone stepping closer to White.

"How would you like to celebrate?"

"Oh I have an idea." Price then pulled White against her by his belt and whispered "Make love to me." in his ear. He kissed her soft smooth lips, smearing the tannish lipstick she was wearing. He always enjoyed the warmth of her kiss.

Price smiled as White's scruffy five o'clock shadow tickled her cheeks. She loved ho he was always so passionate when he kissed her. It pleased her to the point where goosebumps formed on her body and she grew wet with anticipation for the events to follow.

White gently brushed her blonde hair behind her ear, each strand sending sensations through his hand. He heard her moan as he pressed himself tighter against her and ran his hand down the small of her back.

Price's body quivered as White kissed along her neck. She wrapped her arms around his head as he kissed around the edge of the black dress she was wearing, grazing over the top of her breasts. She loved how each kiss was preceded by a light bite almost as if the kisses were to make it better.

White moved from one shoulder to the next, sliding off the straps of the silk dress. He watched as it fell delicately to the tile floor after he removed the last strap. As it fell it revealed Price's fully developed beautifully crafted woman body to him.

Price bit her lower lip erotically as White placed his rough hard-worked hands on her hips and kissed along her neck, lightly nibbling on her ear. She always was attracted to his knowledge of how to handle her body just right. She moaned as he kissed around breasts, pulling her bra down to sensually use his tongue to play with her nipple.

White was turned on by the sounds she made as he teased and pleased her body. He ran his fingers towards her back to unhook her bra and slowly remove it. He then held her supple breasts in his hands as he continued to tease her.

Price grew excited as he lifted her onto the bar. She kicked off her heels as he removed her red thong with his teeth. Her breath became heavy as he kissed around her bellybutton and inner thighs before finally settling on the area in which her legs meet and her body ends.

White felt her fingers combing and pulling his dirty blonde hair as he proceeded to orally please her.

He grew warm with arousal as she moaned uncontrollably and tensed around him.

She could feel her climax growing closer as his wet warm tongue continued to play with her clitoris and lightly enter inside her. Soon she began convulsing erotically until she felt the intense burst of pleasure. Her body shook as the orgasm continued for several seconds. "Now let me please you." She said pulling his head up and kissing him. She enjoyed the feel of his tongue in her mouth when they kissed. She got off the counter and pushed him back against, kissing along his body.

White closed his eyes as Price kissed along the collar of the white button up shirt he was wearing. Then he watched as she unfastened each button and replaced it with a wet kiss. She continued this process for each button. After the last button had been replaced by her lips touching his body, White kissed her as he removed his shirt.

Price loved the feel of his skin on her lips as she kissed down his chest and over his pectoral muscles. She heard a small moan escape him as she toyed with his nipple while unbuckling his belt and pants.

White closed his eyes and titled his head back in pleasure as he felt her moving down his body.

Price slowly removed his pants and underwear allowing his erection that had been bulging in his pants to be free. She then watched as he bit his lower lip while she ran her tongue up the length of his penis. After reaching the tip after the seventh inch she cupped her mouth around it and slowly moved back down to the base.

White felt a sense of ecstasy as he felt the wet warmth of the inside of her mouth envelope the whole length of his penis and then retract to the tip. He was careful not to pull her hair and press her head down for he knew it made her feel sick.

Price could feel the pulsations of White's manhood in her mouth as she moved back down to the base of it. After a minute of stroking him she released his erection and licked up the length of his body up to his mouth where they embraced in another passionate kiss.

White could feel his penis resting in between her warm thighs still erect. He then gently took her to the floor where he stroked her body with his fingers, feeling the goosebumps rise under the tips of each finger. He slowly positioned himself between her legs. Then he felt her grip the base of his cock and insert it inside her. He was overwhelmed by the warm wet silky feeling of her vagina.

Price moaned as she wrapped her legs around White and pulled him deeper inside her. "Take me." She said nibbling his ear lobe. She shrieked in pleasure as White began to thrust inside her. "Oh God Yes!"

She moaned feeling a sense of climax with every inch of him inside her.

White bit his lip as he moved his hips feeling her tighten around him in orgasm. He moaned as she drug her red fingernails down his back leaving a trail of scars behind them.

"Harder!" she screamed causing his thrusts to become more rampant and harder. "Oh John!" she called as another orgasm passed over her. Before either of them knew it thirty minutes had gone by and it was now one in the morning. White finally felt his orgasm reaching the tip of his erect muscle as he continued to move in and out of Price.

"I'm going to cum." White said as she tightened around him.

"Me too!" she proclaimed in a scream of pleasure.

Then in one burst the two climaxed together and collapsed into each other's arms. "That was amazing." Price said in between her and White's heavy breathing.

"You were amazing." White replied embracing her. Price looked at him and wanted to tell him that she had fallen in love with him but was afraid of his response. Then White turned to her and said "I haven't felt this way towards someone since Donna. Jacklyn I do believe I've fallen in love with you." And with that she kissed him and told him that she felt the same. The two then fell asleep right there on the kitchen floor.

It wasn't long before White was woken up by the flash of headlights in the window. He arose and quickly put his pants back on then headed to the front door. He looked out the peephole and saw Anna running up to the door with the bag she packed to stay overnight with her friend.

White opened the door and was immediately met by her embracing his legs in a warm hug. He knelt down and wrapped his arms around her while asking "What happened Princess?"

"I missed you." She said with tears in her eyes.

"Oh sweetheart it's okay. I'm here now."

"I don't want to be away from you again Daddy." She whimpered.

"I promise Anna I will never leave you alone again."

Chapter Five

Section A:

Reconnaissance

Price awoke to the heat of the mid-morning sun filling the small one person tent. She could feel a bead of sweat running across her forehead as she arose from the sleeping bag. After taking a drink of water she ventured outside and found there wasn't much of a temperature change from the inside of the tent.

She proceeded to remove the sleeping bag and dismantle the tent. After she was finished and the equipment was secured in her rucksack she looked around for Hood, who's things had already been packed and was sitting on the ground next to her. Finally she found him standing a little ways away on top of a hill looking through his binoculars.

She threw her bag on her shoulder, then grabbed his and headed towards him. "See anything?" she asked reaching him.

"Not really." He answered as he noticed her carrying his bag. "Oh, thank you."

"No problem." She placed the ruck at his feet and scanned the horizon with her eyes. The sun shown on her face, magnifying the brown coloring of her eyes.

"Just the desert." Hood said putting his binoculars back into his cargo pocket. "Ready to continue on our journey?"

"Yes sir." Price replied turning towards him.

"Great. Follow me." He turned, putting on his ruck, and started walking in the direction of Jericho.

"So you knew Brock?" Price asked trying to keep her mind from worrying about White too much.

"Yeah we trained together back in Officer School." Hood responded stepping around a large rock. "He was a humanitarian then as well."

"What was he like?"

"Young like the rest of us were. Though different in the way he saw people. I always envied his ability to see the good in people."

"He never would give up on you." Price said wiping away the

sweat that had built up along her brow-line.

"That's true." Hood agreed. "He always took care of his people. Of all people that he came across."

"I witnessed that first hand. Back when he got me and Staff Sergeant Willis into Fort Jericho."

"Let me guess. He used one of his speeches to do it."

"Yeah," Price smiled. "And once they let us in he punched the guy in charge for trying to keep us out, then picked him back up and took command."

"Sounds like him." Chuckled Hood. "Never could take orders but damn if you didn't want to just follow him into hell cause you knew he was the only one who could bring you back."

"Probably after talking the Devil into releasing everyone else as well." The two erupted in a quick laugh.

"Yeah he was a great leader. I can't believe he's gone."

"He went down fighting." Said Price trying to put Hood at ease.

"And smiling. He loved to smile in the face of danger. He used to say 'It was the one way to humiliate your opponent even if you had lost. It showed you didn't take them seriously.'"

"Sounds like something he'd say." Price responded as they crossed over a hill.

"See that ridge over there?" Asked Hood pointing out in front of them.

"Yeah."

"We'll have a clear view of Jericho from there."

"Perfect." She said slightly increasing her speed.

"He really means a lot to you huh?" Hood responded as he noticed the increase.

"I love...I mean he's a fellow soldier so of course he does."

"Of course." Hood replied noting the slip but not pursuing the subject.

They continued to increase speed as they neared the ridge. "I hope he's okay." She said to herself.

"I'm sure he is." Answered Hood.

"We will soon find out." Price responded as they reached the ridge and could now see all of Jericho. They both pulled out their binoculars. Hood scanned to note the situation while Price immediately began to search for White.

"They really did some damage." Said Hood continuing to scan the Fort.

"There he is." Price announced "He's been captured." She added in a concerned tone as she saw the net covering White. She soon began to feel a sense of uselessness as she watched White get dragged away. For there was nothing she could do for him now but hope he can find a way out.

Chapter Five

Section B:

What We've Become

White's head throbbed with pain as he finally awoke after being knocked unconscious. As his vision returned to normal he saw a small scorpion crawling past his face. He thought for a moment that if it would only sting him this could all be over. He then turned slowly to scan the area for anyone that could help him.

As he turned to look behind him he saw the woman he had save lying dead in the sand. Ants now crawled around the wound left by the hatchet. White felt a sense of failure but also relief as he stared at her pale blank face. Relieved that she would not have to suffer and he wouldn't have to care for her any longer. "I'm sorry." He said turning away.

He could feel his skin burn and harden as the sun rose higher in the sky. He watched as heat radiated off the ground distorting his vision. His lips began to crack and peel as what little moisture that was left in them evaporated. He started to cough and wheeze. His mouth dried as his dehydration worsened.

"Is this how it ends?" he asked himself realizing that he was no longer able to produce sweat or tears. His eyes began to hurt as with each blink they grew dryer and dryer. He could feel a fever rising from inside him.

"Daddy?" He heard in the distance. He looked around rampantly to find the source. Then he saw a figure in the ripples of the air. "Daddy?" it said again.

"Anna?" White replied in a weak voice.

"Daddy is that you?" asked the figure before it was swept away by a Ravager walking up.

"Challenge-Wake." He said as other Ravagers joined him.

"Take-Chief-Now." Replied one grabbing the net. The others soon joined in and began dragging White away in the net.

"Anna?" White said looking around for the figure. During his search he noticed several Ravagers continuing to rape and desecrate the woman he had saved bruised lifeless body. "What have we become?"

The group of Ravagers drug White across the desert floor for several more feet before turning left. As the turned White could see several women being beat and raped while their husbands and children were being eaten alive.

He could feel blood pooling in his tan shirt as the rocks on the ground scraped against his body. He winced in pain as he was drug over a patch of dry grass, each blade felt like a knife. "Daddy?" White heard again and again.

"Anna!" He called in between coughs. He was suddenly blinded by a cloud of sand that a Ravager kicked at him.

"You-Quiet." Said the Ravager turning back and continuing to help drag him. White coughed as the dust entered his lungs. Once his vision returned he could see a group of crows feasting on a pile of human remains.

"Daddy?" He heard once again just before the Ravagers stopped and he heard on yell.

"We-Bring-Challenge!" then he listened as a metallic door opened and someone or something crawl out of it. He struggled to look up to see what was coming but could only see a large pair of feet approaching him. Each step sounded like thunder.

"This-Challenge?" asked the thing in a deep booming voice. White could see scaring and tribal paint covering its feet. Then suddenly the net was removed and he was violently picked up by two Ravagers.

"Look-At-Chief!" ordered one of them as White struggled to keep his head up due to fatigue. "Look!"

"Fuck you." White replied just before he was forced to look by a third Ravager pulling his hair back. He then gazed upon the beast that had crawled from the metal door. Its face scared and painted. Its biceps as large as White's head and its forearms as thick as White's arms. Its chest protruded several inches and its shoulders were the size of heads as well.

A large fresh scar ran up the middle of the creature's massive body. White then looked it to its eyes and saw nothing but madness and darkness, the eyes of someone who has completely given into the evil that is hidden in every man, woman, and child.

"I-Chief." Said the giant. "You-Challenge."

"You-Dead." Mocked White. "I-Kill-You." He smiled making a joke of the monster's speech pattern. Then White felt the Ravagers push on him, launching him towards the goliath. He was met with a thunderous strike from the Chief. The hit sent White to

the ground, there he felt his face
throb and his mouth fill with blood.

Chapter

Five

Section C:

The End of Hope

White struggled to pick himself up. His ears still ringing from the Chief's fist. He finally rose to his feet only to be knocked back down by another powerful strike from the brute. White watched from the ground as the Chief paced in a small circle with his hands raised to draw might from the cheering crowd.

Whit spat out the blood that was filling his mouth and stood back up once again. The Chief turned to see White standing in fighting stance and slowly walked towards him. White went to punch the Chief only to have his hand caught and snapped back. White cried in pain as his wrist was being broken, then was suddenly thrown back to the ground from another hit from the Chief.

The vision in his left eye blurred as it bruised and swelled with blood and pain. As he began to raise up White felt the Chief's enormous foot stomp on his spine, crushing him into the ground. He was then lifted up and hit several more times. After the last hit White began to see flashes as the Chief began to strike him again and again. Each hit brought the image in the flashes closer and closer. Soon a small figure began to form.

As it neared, White could see the figure's blonde hair and short stature. Then as his vision became clear the figure revealed itself to be Anna wearing a white gown and walking towards him. She placed her small hands on his sun-beat cheeks and looked at him with her crystal clear, ocean blue eyes. She opened her mouth and said "Get up Daddy."

"Anna?" White replied confused.

"Daddy you have to beat him. You have to beat the bad man." Then suddenly as if someone was dragging her away, Anna began to disappear from sight. "Get up Daddy!" she yelled just before completely vanishing.

Then everything cleared and White saw the Chief in the distance taunting the crowd. Suddenly a rush of love, misery, and rage surged through White's veins. He jumped up from the ground. "Anna!" he yelled as he charged the Chief with all his might.

Before the Chief could react, White wrapped his arms around his waist. White could feel the muscles in his arms strain and bulge as he lifted the giant from the ground and violently slammed him back down on his back. "I'll kill you!" White howled as he climbed upon the Chief. He felt the pain in his right wrist as he plunged his fingers deep into the Chief's eye sockets until he felt each eye explode around his thumbs.

The Chief then threw White and clenched his head in pain as he arose from the ground. White began to move around and mock the blind Chief in front of the Ravager crowd. More came to witness their once giant and ferocious leader being blinded and mocked by White. "You-Blind-Now." White said avoiding another one of the Chief's blind attacks.

"Our-Chief-Beat?" Asked a Ravager in the crowd. "New-Chief?" asked another as their cheers slowly shifted to White's favor. The Chief roared, enraged by hearing his once loyal tribe turn on him.

"Over hear." White said attracting the blind animal to his location. As the monster reached him, White swiftly dodged the Chief's fist and began striking the scarred area on his chest. White felt as the Chief's ribs broke apart as he struck them.

The Chief cried in pain as White's fists began to open his

wound. White watched as he punched open the brute's body. Blood splattered in his face with each impact. His once blue eyes grew black as White could taste the iron in the Chief's blood as it entered his mouth.

Soon the Chief's stance began to weaken as he lost more and more blood. Seeing his knees shaking White decided to make the final blow. He kicked in the Chief's left knee sending him to the ground with a thunderous boom. White quickly leapt onto him and, with his broken hand, reached inside the Chief's chest through the open scar. He then ripped out the creature's still beating heart and tore it apart with his teeth.

After he was finished, White watched as the Chief's face grew blank and filled with death. The once cheering crowd had grown silent in awe of what they had just witnessed. White tossed the heart to the ground and picked up his knife that had been tossed to him by a Ravager. He then began to carve around the edges of the Chief's face.

The Ravagers watched as White arose soaked in blood and turn towards them with the look of madness in his eyes.

White looked at them as one by one each Ravager knelt before him and began to chant "New-Chief-New-Chief-New-Chief!" over and over growing louder as more chimed in. A crazed smile slowly formed on

White's face as he held up the dead Chief's severed face and placed it on his own while pronouncing with a lion-like roar "Me-New-Chief!" Then he began to chant "Madness-Madness-Madness!" each time throwing his clenched fist in the sky. Soon the Ravagers stood and joined their new chief in his victorious cheer.

Price watched from the ridge as the man she once knew and loved give himself to the madness, becoming the thing they feared most. Mad. Her heart felt as if it too had been ripped from her chest and was replaced with sorrow. Tears flowed from her eyes and escaped the edges of the binoculars to fall to the desert floor.

"We need to go." Hood said putting away his binoculars. "We need to get back. I know a way we might be able to reclaim Jericho."

Price stood silent for a moment unaware of Hood's words and in a broken tear-filled voice said "No. Not you John." Then as if White heard her he, blood curdling roar that both Price and Hood could hear, said

"No-Hope! Madness-Wins-Always!"

To Be Continued...

IN

Fall into Madness
Pt.2

The Return

Special Thanks To:

Brett Scott

Elijah Shomo

Benjamin Wakely

Darrick Willis

Aaron Lawson

Shania Maurey

Mathew Hood

Timothy Clifford

Sean Carlan

Emmanuel Gutierrez

&

Timothy Patterson

Very Special Thanks To:

Darrick Willis

Mathew Hood

&

Timothy Clifford

9 7 9 8 8 3 8 1 6 9 4 5 7